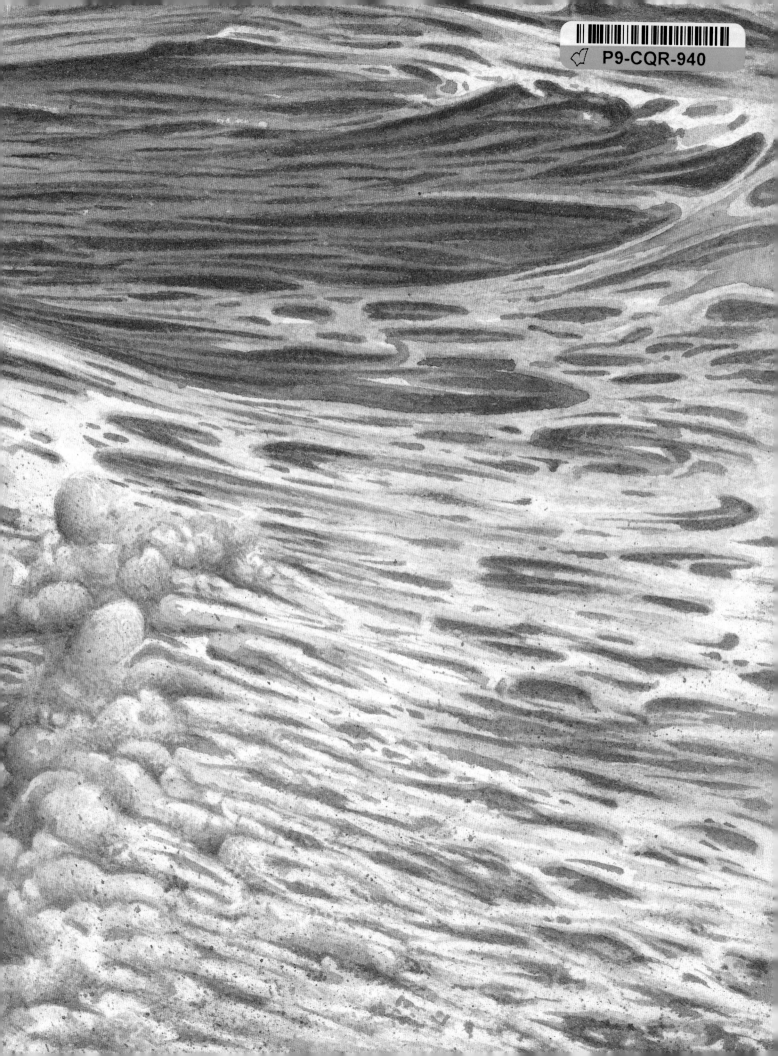

THE LITTLE MERMAID

This book is dedicated to my dear daughter, Christina.

CHARLES SANTORE

Afterword copyright © 1993 by Outlet Book Company, Inc.
Illustrations copyright © 1993 by Charles Santore.

This 1993 edition is published by JellyBean Press,
a division of dilithium Press, Ltd.,
distributed by Outlet Book Company, Inc.,
a Random House Company,
40 Engelhard Avenue, Avenel, New Jersey 07001.

DILITHIUM is a registered trademark and
JELLYBEAN PRESS is a trademark of dilithium Press, Ltd.

Printed and bound in Italy

Book and jacket design by Melissa Ring
Production supervision by Roméo Enriquez

Library of Congress Cataloging-in-Publication Data
Andersen, H.C. (Hans Christian), 1805-1875.
    [Lille havfrue. English]
    The little mermaid : the original story / by Hans Christian
Andersen ; illustrated by Charles Santore.
      p.   cm
    Summary : A little sea princess, longing to be human, trades her
mermaid's tail for legs, hoping to win the love of a prince and earn
an immortal soul for herself.
    ISBN 0-517-06495-2
    [1. Fairy tales, 2. Mermaids—Fiction.] I. Santore, Charles,
ill. II. Title.
PZ8.A542Lit 1993b
[Fic]—dc20
                                  93-20375
                                      CIP
                                      AC

8 7 6 5 4 3 2 1

THE LITTLE MERMAID

The Original Story by
Hans Christian Andersen

Illustrated by
Charles Santore

JellyBean Press
New York · Avenel

Far out at sea, the water is as blue as the prettiest cornflowers, and as clear as the purest crystal. But it is very deep—so deep, indeed, that no rope can measure it, and many church steeples must be piled one upon the other to reach from the bottom to the surface. It is there that the sea folk dwell.

There is not just bare, white, sandy ground below the sea. The soil produces the most curious trees and flowers, whose leaves and stems are so flexible that the slightest motion of the waters seems to stir them as if they were living creatures. Fish, great and small, glide through the branches as birds fly through the trees upon earth. In the deepest spot of all stands the Sea King's palace. Its walls are of coral, and its tall pointed windows of the clearest amber, while the roof is made of mussel shells that open and shut according to the tide. And in each

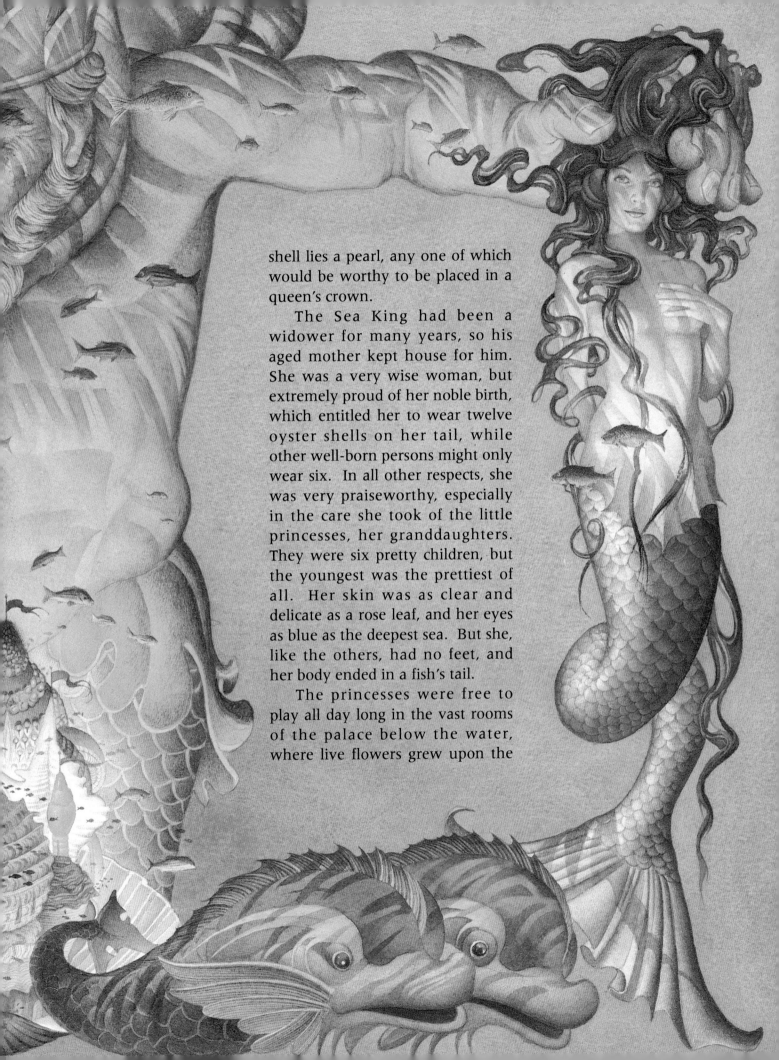

shell lies a pearl, any one of which would be worthy to be placed in a queen's crown.

The Sea King had been a widower for many years, so his aged mother kept house for him. She was a very wise woman, but extremely proud of her noble birth, which entitled her to wear twelve oyster shells on her tail, while other well-born persons might only wear six. In all other respects, she was very praiseworthy, especially in the care she took of the little princesses, her granddaughters. They were six pretty children, but the youngest was the prettiest of all. Her skin was as clear and delicate as a rose leaf, and her eyes as blue as the deepest sea. But she, like the others, had no feet, and her body ended in a fish's tail.

The princesses were free to play all day long in the vast rooms of the palace below the water, where live flowers grew upon the

walls. When the large amber windows were opened, the fish would swim in right up to the princesses. They ate out of their hands, and allowed themselves to be stroked.

In front of the palace there was a large garden with bright red and dark blue trees, whose fruit glittered like gold, and whose blossoms were like fiery sparks. The ground was strewn with the most delicate sand, but it was as blue as the flames of sulphur. The whole atmosphere

was of a peculiar blue tint, as if you were hovering high up in the air, with clouds above and below, rather than standing at the bottom of the sea. When the winds were calm, the sun was visible, and to those below it looked like a scarlet flower shedding light.

Each of the little princesses had a plot of ground in the garden, where she might dig and plant as she pleased. One sowed her flowers so they would come up in the shape of a whale. Another preferred the figure of a little mermaid. But the youngest planted hers in a circle to imitate the sun, and chose flowers as red as the sun appeared to her. She was a singular

child, both silent and thoughtful, and while her sisters were delighted with all the strange things that they obtained from the wrecks of various ships, she had never claimed anything except a pretty statue of a handsome youth, hewn out of pure white marble, that had sunk to the bottom of the sea when a ship ran aground. Beside the statue there was a beautiful red seaweed tree. When the tree grew up, its fresh boughs hung over it nearly down to the blue sands, where the shadow looked quite violet, and kept dancing about like the branches. It seemed as if the top of the tree were at play with its roots, each trying to snatch a kiss.

There was nothing the youngest princess delighted in so much as to hear about the upper world. She was always asking her grandmother to tell her all she knew about ships, towns, people, and animals. What struck her as most wonderful was that the flowers of the earth should shed perfumes, which they do not below the sea, that the forests were green, and that the fish among the trees should sing so loud and so exquisitely that it must be a treat to hear them. (It was the little birds that her grandmother called "fish," or else her young listeners would not have understood her, for they had never seen birds.)

"When you have reached your fifteenth year," said the grandmother, "you shall be allowed to rise up out of the sea, and sit on the rocks in the moonlight, and look at the large ships sailing past. And then you will see both forests and towns."

In the following year one of the sisters would reach the age of fifteen, but as all the rest were each a year younger than the other, the youngest would have to wait five years before it would be her turn to come up from the bottom of the ocean, and see what the world was like. The eldest, however, promised to tell the others what she saw, and what struck her as most beautiful on the first day, for their grandmother did not tell them enough, and there were so many things they wanted to know.

But none of them longed for her turn to come so intensely as did the youngest, who had to wait the longest, and was so reserved and thoughtful. Many a night she stood at the open window, and gazed upward through the dark blue water, and watched the fish as

they lashed the sea with their fins and tails. She could see the moon and stars, which appeared rather pale, though much larger, seen through the water, than they do to us. If something resembling a black cloud glided between the stars and herself, she knew that it was either a whale swimming overhead, or a ship full of human beings, none of whom probably dreamed that a lovely little mermaid was standing below, and stretching forth her white hands toward the keel of their vessel.

The eldest princess was now fifteen, and was allowed to rise up to the surface of the sea.

On her return she had a great deal to relate, but the most delightful thing of all, she said, was to lie upon a sand-bank in the calm sea, and to gaze upon the large city near the coast, where lights were shining like hundreds of stars; to listen to the sounds of music,

the din of carriages, and the busy hum of the crowd; and to see the church steeples, and hear the bells ringing. And she longed after all these things, just because she could not approach them.

Oh, how attentively her youngest sister listened! And later in the evening, when she stood at the open window, and gazed up through the dark blue water, how she thought about the large city, with its din and bustle, and even fancied she could hear the church bells ringing.

In the following year, the second sister was given permission to rise up to the surface of the water and swim about at her pleasure. She went up just at sunset, which appeared to her the finest sight of all. She said that the whole sky appeared like gold, and as to the clouds, their beauty was beyond all description. Red and violet clouds sailed rapidly above her head, while a

flock of wild swans, resembling a long white scarf, flew still faster than the clouds across the sea toward the setting sun. She, too, swam toward it, but the sun sank down, and the rosy hues vanished from the surface of the water and from the skies.

The year after, the third sister went up. She was the boldest of them all, so she swam up a river that emptied into the sea. She saw beautiful green hills covered with vines. Castles and citadels peeped out from stately woods. She heard the birds singing, and the sun felt so warm that she was frequently obliged to dive down under the water to cool her burning face. In a small creek she met with a whole troop of human children. They were naked, and dabbling about in the water. She wanted to play with them, but they ran away in great alarm, and there came a little black animal (she meant a dog, only she had never seen one before),

who barked at her so tremendously that she was frightened, and sought to reach the open sea. But she thought she would never forget the beautiful forests, the green hills, or the pretty children, who were able to swim in the water although they had no fish tails.

The fourth sister was less daring. She remained in the midst of the sea, and maintained that it was most beautiful at that point, because from there she could see for miles around, and the sky looked like a glass bell above her head. She had seen ships, but only at a distance—they looked like seagulls, and the playful dolphins had turned somersaults, and the large whales had squirted water through their nostrils, so that one might fancy there were hundreds of fountains all around.

It was now the fifth sister's turn. Her birthday was in the winter, therefore she saw what the others had

not seen the first time they went up. The sea looked quite green, and huge icebergs were floating about. Each looked like a pearl, she said, only larger than the churches built by human beings. They were of the oddest shapes, and glittered like diamonds. She had placed herself upon the largest of them, letting the wind play with her long hair, and all the ships scudded past in great alarm, as though fearful of approaching the spot where she was sitting. Toward evening, the sky became overcast, with thunder and lightning, while the dark sea lifted up the huge icebergs, so that they were illuminated by the red flashes of the lightning. All the ships reefed in their sails, and their passengers were panic-stricken, while the mermaid sat quietly on her floating block of ice and watched the lightning as it zigzagged along the silent sea.

The first time that each of the sisters had risen to the surface of the water, they had been enchanted by the novelty and beauty of all they saw. But being now grown up, and at liberty to go above as often as they pleased, they had grown indifferent to such excursions. They longed to come back into the sea, and, at the end of a month, they had all declared that it was far more beautiful down below, and that it was more pleasant to stay at home.

Frequently, in the evening, the five older sisters would entwine their arms, and rise up to the surface of the water all in a row. They had beautiful voices, far finer than any human being's, and when a storm was coming on, and they anticipated that a ship might sink, they swam before it, and sang most sweetly of the delights to be found beneath the water, begging the seafarers not to be afraid of coming down below. But the sailors could not understand what they said, and mistook their words for the howling of the tempest. They never saw all the fine things below, for, if the ship sank,

the men were always drowned, and their bodies alone reached the Sea King's palace.

When the sisters rose up arm in arm through the water, the youngest would stand alone, looking after them, and felt ready to cry; only mermaids have no tears, and therefore suffer all the more.

"How I wish I were fifteen!" said she. "I am sure I shall love the world above, and the beings that inhabit it."

At last she reached the age of fifteen.

"Well, now you are grown up!" said her grandmother. "So let me dress you like your sisters." And she placed in her hair a wreath of white lilies, every leaf of which was half a pearl. And the old lady ordered eight large oyster shells to be fastened to the princess's tail, to denote her high rank.

"But they hurt me so," said the little mermaid.

"Pride must suffer pain," said the old lady.

Oh! How gladly would the little mermaid have shaken off all this pomp and laid aside her heavy wreath—the red flowers in her garden adorned her far better—but she had no choice. "Farewell!" she cried, rising lightly to the surface of the water.

The sun had just sunk as she raised her head above the waves, but the clouds were still pink, and fringed with gold. And through the fast vanishing rosy tints of the air

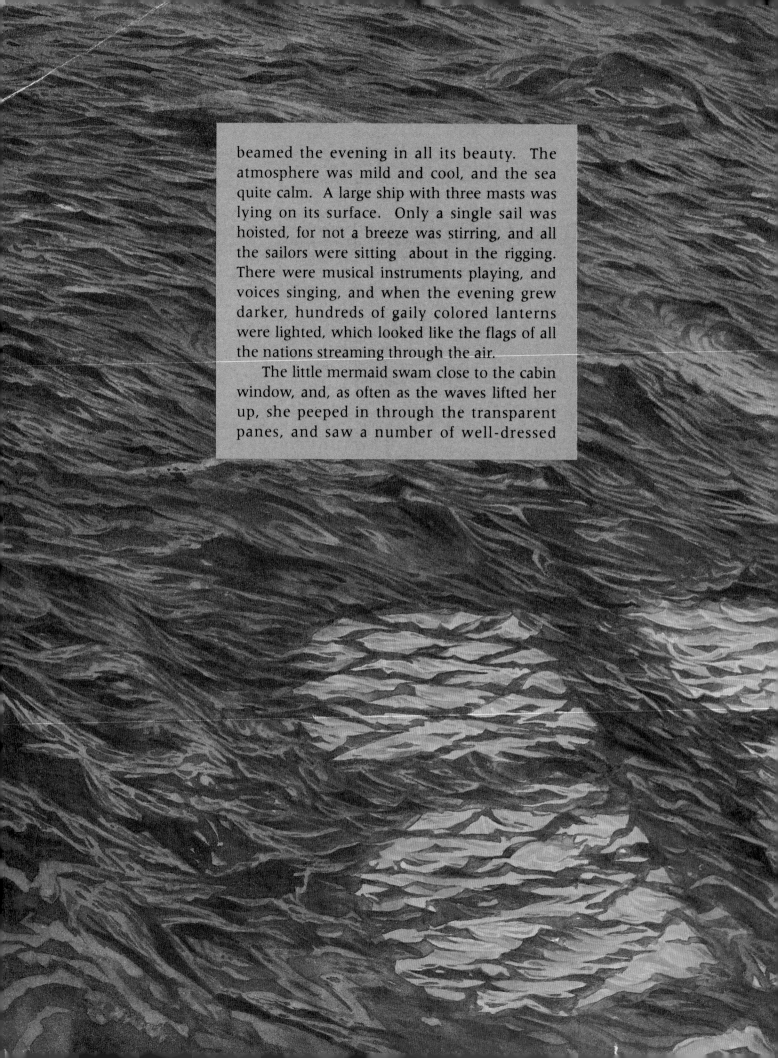

beamed the evening in all its beauty. The atmosphere was mild and cool, and the sea quite calm. A large ship with three masts was lying on its surface. Only a single sail was hoisted, for not a breeze was stirring, and all the sailors were sitting about in the rigging. There were musical instruments playing, and voices singing, and when the evening grew darker, hundreds of gaily colored lanterns were lighted, which looked like the flags of all the nations streaming through the air.

The little mermaid swam close to the cabin window, and, as often as the waves lifted her up, she peeped in through the transparent panes, and saw a number of well-dressed

people. But the handsomest of all was the prince, with large, dark eyes. He could not have been more than sixteen, and it was his birthday that was being celebrated with such magnificence. The sailors danced upon the deck, and when the young prince came up, a hundred rockets were set off, which lit the air until it was as bright as day, and so frightened the little mermaid that she dived under the water. But she soon popped her head up once more, when all the stars in heaven seemed to be falling down upon her. She had never seen fireworks before; large suns were throwing out sparks, beautiful fiery fish were darting through the blue air, and all these wonders were reflected in the calm sea below. The ship itself was thrown into such bright relief that every little cord was distinctly visible, and, of course, each person even more so. And how handsome the young prince looked, as he pressed the hands of those present and smiled, while the music resounded through that lovely night.

It was late. Still, the little mermaid could not take her eyes off the ship or the handsome prince. The many-colored lanterns were now extinguished, the rockets ceased to be set off, and no more cannons were fired. But there was a rumbling and a grumbling in the heart of the sea. Still she sat rocking up and down in the water, so as to peep

into the cabin. But now the ship began to move faster. The sails were unfurled one after another. The waves ran higher. Heavy clouds flitted across the sky, and flashes of lightning were seen in the distance. A tremendous storm seemed to be coming on, so the sailors reefed in the sails once more. The large ship kept pitching to and fro in its rapid course across the raging sea. The billows heaved, like so many gigantic black mountains, threatening to roll over the topmast, but the ship dived down like a swan between the high waves, and then rose again on the towering pinnacle of the waters. The little mermaid fancied this was a pleasant mode of sailing, but the crew thought differently.

The ship kept cracking and cracking, the thick planks gave way beneath the repeated lashings of the waves, a leak was sprung, the mast was broken in two like a reed, and the vessel drooped on one side, while the water kept filling the hold.

The little mermaid now realized that the crew were in danger, and she herself was obliged to take care not to be hurt by the ship's beams and planks that were dispersed upon the water. For one moment, it was so dark that she could see nothing, but when a flash of lightning illuminated the sky, and enabled her to discern distinctly all on board, she looked especially for the young prince whom she saw sinking into

the water just as the ship burst asunder.

She was quite pleased at the thought of his coming down to her, until she reflected that human beings cannot live in water, and that he would be dead by the time he reached her father's castle. But die he must not, therefore she swam toward him through the planks and beams that were driven about on the billows, forgetting that they might crush her to atoms. She dived deep under the water, and then, rising again between the waves, she managed at length to

reach the young prince, who was scarcely able to cope any longer with the stormy sea. His arms and legs began to feel powerless, his beautiful eyes were closed, and he would have died had not the little mermaid come to his assistance. She held his head above the water, and then let the waves carry them.

Toward morning the storm had abated, but the wreck of the ship was not to be seen. The sun rose red and beaming from the water, and seemed to infuse life into the prince's cheeks, but his eyes remained closed. The mermaid kissed his high, polished forehead, and stroked back his wet hair. She fancied he was like the marble statue in her garden, and she kissed him again, and wished that he might live.

They now came in sight of land, and she saw high blue mountains, on the tops of which the snow looked as dazzlingly white as though a flock of swans were lying there. Below, near the coast, were beautiful green forests, and in front stood a large white building. Lemons and oranges grew in the garden, and tall palm trees stood in front of the door. The sea formed a small bay at this spot, and the water, though very deep, was quite calm. She swam with the handsome prince toward the cliff, where the delicate white sands had formed a heap, and here she laid him down in the warm sunshine, taking great care that his head should be placed higher than his body.

The bells now pealed from the white building, and a number of girls came into the garden. The little mermaid then swam a short distance away and hid herself behind some high stones that rose out of the water so that no one could see her, and she watched to see whether anyone would come to the poor prince's assistance.

It was not long before a young maiden approached the spot where he was lying. She appeared frightened at first, but it was only for a moment; and then she fetched a number of people and the mermaid saw that the prince came to life again, and that he smiled at all those around him. But he did not send her a smile, neither did he know that she had saved him, so

she felt quite sad. And when he was led into the large building she dived back into the water with a heavy heart and returned to her father's castle.

Silent and thoughtful as she had always been, she now grew even more so. Her sisters inquired what she had seen the first time she went above, but she did not tell.

Many an evening, and many a morning, did she rise up to the spot where she had left the prince. She saw the fruit in the garden grow ripe, and then she saw it gathered. She saw the snow melt away from the summits of the high mountains, but she did not see the prince. And each time she returned home more sorrowful than ever. Her only consolation was to sit in her little garden and to fling her arm around the beautiful marble statue that was like the prince. But she ceased to tend to her flowers, and they grew like a wilderness all over the paths, entwining their long stems and leaves with the branches of the trees, so that it was quite dark beneath their shade.

At length she could resist no longer, and opened her heart to one of her sisters, from whom all the others immediately learned her secret, though they told it to no one else, except to a couple of other mermaids, who divulged it to nobody, except to their closest friends. One of these happened to know who the prince was. She, too, had seen the gala on shipboard, and told them from whence he came, and where his kingdom lay.

"Come, little sister," said the other princesses, and, entwining their arms, they rose up in a long row out of the sea at the spot where they knew the prince's palace stood.

The palace was built of bright yellow, shining stone, with a broad flight of marble steps, the last of which reached down into the sea.

Now that the little mermaid knew where the prince lived, she spent many an evening, and many a night, in the neighboring waters. She swam much nearer to the

shore than any of the others had ventured to do. She even went up the narrow canal, under the handsome marble balcony that threw its long shadow over the water. Here she would sit and gaze at the young prince, who thought himself quite alone in the bright moonlight.

Many an evening did she see him sailing in his pretty boat, adorned with flags, and enjoying music. Then she would listen from among the green reeds. And if the wind happened to seize hold of her long silvery white veil, those who saw it took it to be a swan spreading his wings.

Many a night, too, when fishermen were spreading their nets by torchlight, she heard them speaking highly of the young prince, and she rejoiced that she had saved his life, when he was tossed about, half dead, on the waves. And she remembered how his head had rested on her bosom, and how heartily she had kissed him. But of all this he knew nothing, and he could not even dream about her.

She soon grew to be more and more fond of human beings, and to long more and more fervently to be able to walk about among them, for their world appeared to her far larger and more beautiful than her own. They could fly across the sea in their ships, and scale mountains that towered above the clouds. And the lands they possessed—their fields and their forests—stretched far away beyond the reach of her sight.

There was such a great deal that the little mermaid wanted to learn, but her sisters were not able to answer all her questions. Therefore, she went to her old grandmother, who was well acquainted with the upper world, which she called the lands above the sea.

"If human beings do not drown," asked the little mermaid, "can they live forever? Do they not die, as we do here in the sea?"

"Yes," said the ancient dame, "they must die as well as we. And the term of their life is even shorter than ours. We can live to be three hundred years old. But when we cease to be here, we shall only be changed into foam, and are not even buried below among those we love. And our souls are not

immortal; we shall never enter upon a new life. We are like the green reed that can never flourish again when it has once been cut through. Human beings, on the contrary, have a soul that lives eternally—yes, even after the body has been committed to the earth—and that rises up through the clear, pure air to the bright stars above! As we rise out of the water to look at the haunts of men, so do they rise to unknown and favored regions, which we shall never be privileged to see."

"And why do we not have immortal souls?" asked the little mermaid sorrowfully. "I would willingly give all the hundreds of years I may have to live, to be a human being for but one day, and to have the hope of sharing in the joys of the heavenly world."

"You must not think about that," said the old lady. "We feel we are much happier and better than the human race above."

"So I shall die, and be driven about like foam on the sea, and cease to hear the music of the waves, and to see the beautiful flowers, and the red sun? Is there nothing I can do to obtain an immortal soul?"

"No," said the old sea queen, "unless a human being loved you so dearly that you were more to him than either father or mother. If all his thoughts and his love were centered in you, and he allowed the priest to lay his right hand in yours, promising to be faithful to you here and hereafter, then would his soul glide into your body, and you would obtain a share in the happiness awaiting human beings. He would give you a soul without forfeiting his own. But this will never happen! Your fish's tail, which is beautiful to us sea folk, is thought a deformity on earth, because they know no better. It is necessary there to have two stout props, which they call legs, to be beautiful!"

The little mermaid sighed as she cast a glance at her fish's tail.

"Let us be merry," said the old lady. "Let us jump and swim about during the three hundred years that we have to live—which is really quite enough. We shall then be all the more disposed to rest later. Tonight we shall have a court ball."

On the occasions of a court ball there was a display of magnificence such as is never seen upon earth. The walls and the ceiling of the large ballroom were of thick, though transparent, glass. Hundreds of colossal mussel shells—some of a deep red, others as green as grass—were hung in rows on each side, and contained blue flames, which illuminated the whole room and shone through the walls so that the sea was lighted all around. Countless fish, great and small, were to be seen swimming past the glass walls, some of them flaunting scarlet scales, while others sparkled like liquid gold or silver.

Through the ballroom flowed a wide stream, on whose surface the mermen and mermaids danced to their own sweet singing. Human beings have no such voices. The little mermaid sang the sweetest of them all, and the whole court applauded with their hands and tails. For a moment she felt delighted, for she knew that she had the loveliest voice ever heard upon earth or upon the sea. But her thoughts soon turned once more to the upper world, for she could not long forget either the handsome prince or her grief at not having an immortal soul like his. She, therefore, stole out of her father's palace, where all was song and festivity, and went to sit sadly in her own little garden. Then she heard a bugle sounding through the water.

Now, she thought, he is surely sailing about up above—he who incessantly fills all my thoughts, and to whose hands I would with pleasure entrust the happiness of my existence. I will venture everything to win him and to obtain an immortal soul. While my sisters are dancing in my father's castle, I will go to the Sea Witch. She has always frightened me, but now, perhaps, she can advise and help me.

The little mermaid left her garden and went to the rushing whirlpool, behind which the sorceress lived. She had never gone there before. Neither flowers nor sea grass grew there. Nothing but bare, sandy ground led to the whirlpool, where the waters kept eddying like waving mill wheels, dragging everything they clutched down into the fathomless depth below. The little

mermaid was forced to pass between these whirlpools, which might very well have crushed her in their rude grasp, to reach the dominion of the Sea Witch. And even here, during a good part of the way, there was no other road than across a sheet of warm, bubbling mire, which the witch called her turf. At the back of this lay her house, in the midst of a most unusual forest. Its trees and bushes were polypi—half animal, half plant—and they looked like hundred-headed serpents growing out of the ground. The branches were long, slimy arms, with fingers like flexible worms, and they could move every joint from the root to the tip. They held fast to whatever they could snatch from the sea, and never yielded it up again. The little mermaid was so frightened at the sight of them that her heart beat with fear. She wanted to turn back, but then she thought of the prince, and of the soul that human beings possessed, and she took courage. She knotted her long, flowing hair, that the polypi might not seize hold of her locks, and, crossing her hands over her bosom, she darted along, as a fish shoots through the water, between the ugly polypi that stretched out their flexible arms and fingers behind her. She saw how each of them retained what it had seized, with hundreds of little arms as strong as iron clasps. Human beings, who had died at sea and had sunk below, looked like white skeletons in the arms of the polypi. They clutched rudders, too, and chests, and skeletons of animals belonging to the earth, and even a little mermaid whom they had caught—and this seemed to her to be the most shocking of all.

She now approached a vast swamp in the forest, where large, fat water snakes were wallowing in the mire and displaying their ugly whitish-yellow bodies. In the midst of this loathsome spot stood a house, built of the bones of shipwrecked human beings. Within it sat the Sea Witch, feeding a toad. She called the snakes her "little chicks," and let them creep all over her.

"I know what you want!" said the Sea Witch. "It is very stupid of you, but you shall have your way, even though it will plunge you into misfortune.

My fair princess, you want to be rid of your fish's tail, and to have a couple of props like those human beings have to walk about upon, so that the young prince may fall in love with you, and so that you may obtain his hand and an immortal soul into the bargain!" And then the old witch laughed so loud and so repulsively that the toad and the snakes fell to the ground, where they lay wriggling about. "You come just in the nick of time," added the witch, "for tomorrow, by sunrise, I should no longer be able to help you until another year had flown past. I will prepare a potion for you. You must swim ashore with it tomorrow, before sunrise, and then sit down and drink it. Your tail will then disappear, and shrivel up into what human beings call legs. But mind, it will hurt you as much as if a sharp sword were thrust through you. Everybody that sees you will say you are the most beautiful mortal ever seen. You will keep the floating elegance of your movement. No dancer will move so lightly as you, but every step you take will be like treading upon such sharp knives that you would think your blood must flow. If you choose to put up with sufferings like these, I have the power to help you."

"I do," said the little mermaid, in a trembling voice, as she thought of the prince and of an immortal soul.

"But think you well," said the witch. "If once you obtain a human form, you can never be a mermaid again! You will never be able to dive down into the water to your sisters or return to your father's palace. And if you should fail to win the prince's love to the degree of his forgetting both father and mother for your sake, and loving you with his whole soul, and bidding the priest to join your hands in marriage, then you will never obtain an immortal soul! And the very day after he will have married another, your heart will break, and you will dissolve into the foam on the billows."

"I am resolved," said the little mermaid, who had turned as pale as death.

"But you must pay me my dues," said the witch, "and it is no small matter I require. You have the loveliest voice of all the inhabitants of the deep, and you reckon upon its tones to charm him into loving you. Now, you must give

me this beautiful voice. I choose to have the best of all you possess in exchange for my valuable potion. For I must mix my own blood with it, that it may prove as sharp as a two-edged sword."

"But if you take away my voice," said the little mermaid, "what have I left?"

"Your lovely form," said the witch, "your buoyant carriage, and your expressive eyes. With these you surely can capture a man's heart. Well? Has your courage melted away? Come, put out your little tongue, and let me take it for my fee, and you shall have the valuable potion."

"So be it," said the little mermaid, and the witch put her cauldron on the fire to prepare the potion. "Cleanliness is a virtue!" she said, scouring the cauldron with the snakes that she had tied into a knot; after which she pricked her own skin, and let her black blood trickle down into the vessel. The steam rose up in such fanciful shapes that no one could have looked at them without a shudder. But when the potion was ready, it looked like the purest spring water.

"Here it is," said the witch, taking the mermaid's tongue, so that now she could neither sing nor speak.

"If the polypi should seize hold of you on your return through my forest," said the witch, "you need only sprinkle a single drop of this potion over them, and their arms and fingers will be shattered into a thousand pieces." But the little mermaid had no need of this talisman. The polypi drew back in alarm from her on perceiving the dazzling potion that shone in her hand like a twinkling star. So she crossed rapidly through the forest, the swamp, and the raging whirlpool.

She saw her father's palace, where the torches were now extinguished in the large ballroom, and she knew the whole family was asleep within, but she did not dare venture to go and seek them, now that she could not speak and was about to leave them forever. Her heart seemed ready to burst with anguish. She stole into the garden and plucked a flower from each of her

sisters' flowerbeds, threw a thousand kisses to the palace, and then rose up through the blue waters.

The sun had not yet risen when she saw the prince's castle and reached the magnificent marble steps. The moon shone brightly. The little mermaid drank the sharp and burning potion, and it seemed as if a two-edged sword was run through her delicate frame. She fainted away, and remained apparently lifeless.

When the sun rose over the sea she awoke, and felt a sharp pang, but just before her stood the handsome young prince. He gazed at her so intently with his coal-black eyes that she cast her eyes to the ground, and now saw that her fish's tail had disappeared, and that she had a pair of the nicest little white legs that a maiden could desire. Only, having no clothes on, she was obliged to wrap herself in her long, thick hair. The prince asked who she was, and how she had come there, but she could only look at him with her mild but sorrowful deep blue eyes, for she could not speak. He

then took her by the hand, and led her into the palace. Every step she took was, as the witch had warned her, like treading on the points of needles and sharp knives, but she bore it willingly, and, hand in hand with the prince, she glided in as lightly as a soap bubble, so that he, as well as everybody else, marveled at her lovely airy gait.

The little mermaid was dressed in costly robes of silk and muslin, and was the most beautiful of all the women in the palace, but she could neither sing nor speak. Handsome women, attired in silk and gold, came and sang before the prince and his royal parents. One of them sang more beautifully than all the others and the prince clapped his hands and smiled. This saddened the little mermaid. She knew that she herself had sung much more exquisitely, and thought, If he but knew that to be near him I sacrificed my voice for all eternity!

The women now performed a variety of elegant dances to the sound of the most delightful music. The little mermaid then raised her beautiful white arms, stood on the

tips of her toes, and floated across the floor in such a way as no one had ever danced before. Every motion revealed some fresh beauty, and her eyes appealed still more directly to the heart than the singing of the women had done.

Everybody was enchanted, but most of all the prince, who called her his little foundling. She danced on and on, though every time her foot touched the floor she felt as if she were treading on sharp knives. The prince declared that he would never part with her, and allowed her to sleep on a velvet cushion before his door.

He had her dressed in male attire, that she might accompany him on horseback, and they rode together through the perfumed forests, where the green boughs touched

their shoulders, and the little birds sang among the cool leaves.
She climbed mountains at the prince's side, and though her
tender feet bled so that others noticed it, she only laughed at her
sufferings, and followed him until they could see the clouds
rolling beneath them like a flock of birds bound for some distant
land.

At night, when others throughout the prince's palace slept, she would go
and sit on the broad marble steps, for it cooled her burning feet to bathe them in
the sea water. It was then she thought of those below in the deep.

One night her sisters rose up arm in arm, and sang mournfully as they glided over
the waters. She then made them a sign. When they recognized her, they told her how
deeply she had saddened them all. After that they visited her every night. And once
she saw at a great distance her aged grandmother, who had not come up above the
surface of the sea for many years, and the Sea King, with his crown on his head. They
stretched out their arms to her, but they did not venture as near the shore as her
sisters.

Each day the little mermaid grew to love the prince more fondly and he loved her
just as one loves a dear, good child. But as to choosing her for his queen, such an idea
never entered his head. Yet, unless she became his wife, she would not obtain an
immortal soul, and would melt to foam on the day after his wedding to another.

"Don't you love me the best of all?" the little mermaid's eyes would seem to ask
when he embraced her and kissed her fair forehead.

"Yes, I love you best," said the prince, "for you have the best heart of any. You are
the most devoted to me, and you resemble a young maiden whom I once saw, but
whom I shall never meet again. I was on board a ship that sank, and the billows cast
me near a holy temple, where several young maidens were performing divine services.

The youngest of them found me on the shore and saved my life. I saw her only twice. She would be the only one that I could love in this world. But your features are like hers, and you have almost driven her image out of my soul. She belongs to the holy temple, and therefore, my good star has sent you to me—and we will never part."

Alas! He knows not that it was I who saved his life, thought the little mermaid. I carried him across the sea to the wood where the holy temple stands, and I sat beneath the foam to watch whether any human being came to help him. I saw the pretty girl whom he loves better than he does me. And the mermaid heaved a deep sigh, for she had no tears to shed, and she reflected, He says the maiden belongs to the holy temple, and she will, therefore, never return to the world. They will not meet again and I am by his side and see him every day. I will take care of him, and love him, and sacrifice my life for him.

But now came talk of the prince being about to marry, and to take for his wife the beautiful daughter of a neighboring king. That was why he was fitting out a magnificent vessel. The prince was traveling ostensibly on a mere visit to his neighbor's estates, but in reality to see the king's daughter. He was to be accompanied by a large retinue. The little mermaid shook her head and smiled. She knew the prince's thoughts better than the others did. "I must travel," he had said to her. "I must see this beautiful princess, because my parents require it of me, but they will not force me to bring her home as my bride. I cannot love her. She will not resemble the beautiful maiden in the temple whom you are like. And if I were compelled to choose a bride, it should sooner be you, my mute foundling, with those expressive eyes of yours." And he kissed her rosy mouth, and rested his head against her heart, which beat high with hopes of human felicity and of an immortal soul.

"You are not afraid of the sea, my child, are you?" said he, as they stood on the magnificent vessel that was to carry them to the neighboring king's dominions. And he talked to her about tempests and calm, of the singular fish to be found in the deep, and of the wonderful things the divers saw below. She smiled, for she knew better than anyone else what was in the sea below.

During the moonlit night, when all were asleep on board, even the helmsman at his rudder, she sat on deck, and gazed through the clear waters, and fancied she saw her father's palace. High above it stood her aged grand-mother, with her silver crown on her head, looking up intently at the keel of the ship. Then her sisters rose to the surface, and gazed at her mournfully, and wrung their white hands. She made a sign to them, smiled, and would have liked to have told them that she was happy and well off, but the cabin boy approached, and the sisters dived beneath the waves, leaving him to believe that the white forms he thought he saw were only the foam upon the billowing waters.

Next morning the ship came into port at the neighboring king's splendid capital. The bells were all set to ringing, trumpets sounded flourishes from high turrets, and soldiers, with flying colors and shining bayonets, stood ready to welcome the stranger.

Every day brought some new entertainment: balls and feasts succeeded each other. But the princess was not yet there. She had been brought up, people said, in a far distant, holy temple, where she had acquired all manner of royal virtues. At last she came.

The little mermaid was obliged to acknowledge to herself that she had never seen a lovelier face. Her skin was delicate and transparent, and beneath her long, dark lashes sparkled sincere, dark blue eyes.

"It is you!" cried the prince. "You saved me, when I lay like a lifeless corpse upon the shore!" And he folded the blushing princess in his arms. "Oh, I am too happy!" he said to the little mermaid. "My fondest dream has come to pass. You will rejoice at my happiness, for you wish me well, more than any of them." And the

little mermaid kissed his hand, and felt already as if her heart was about to break. His wedding morning would bring her death, and she would then be changed to foam upon the sea.

All the church bells were ringing, and the heralds rode through the streets, and proclaimed the approaching nuptials. Perfumed oil was burning in costly silver lamps on all the altars. The priests swung their incense burners while the bride and bridegroom joined their hands and received the bishop's blessing. The little mermaid, dressed in silk and gold, held the bride's train, but her ears did not hear the solemn music, neither did her eyes behold the ceremony. She thought of the approaching gloom of death, and of all she had lost in this world.

That same evening the bride and bridegroom went on board the prince's vessel. The cannons were roaring, the banners were streaming, and a costly tent of gold and purple, lined with cushions, had been prepared on deck for the reception of the bridal pair.

The vessel then set sail, with a favorable wind, and glided smoothly along the calm sea.

When it grew dark, a number of colored lamps were lit, and the crew danced merrily on deck. The little mermaid could not help remembering her first visit to the earth, when she witnessed similar festivities and magnificence. She twirled round in the dance, half poised in the air, like a swallow when pursued, and all present cheered her ecstatically, for never before had she danced so enchantingly. Her tender feet felt the sharp pangs of knives, but she heeded them not, for a sharper pang had shot through her heart. She knew that this was the last evening she should ever be able to see him for whom she had left her family and her home, sacrificed her beautiful voice, and daily suffered the most excruciating pain. It was the last night on which she might breathe the same air as he, and gaze at the deep sea and the starry sky. An eternal night, unenlivened by either thoughts or dreams, now awaited her, for she had no soul, and could now never obtain one. Yet all was joy and gaiety on board until long past midnight; and she laughed and danced, though thoughts of death were in her heart.

The prince kissed his beautiful bride, and she played with his black locks. Then they went, arm in arm, to rest beneath the splendid tent.

All was now quiet on board. Only the steersman was sitting at the helm, as the little mermaid leaned her white arms on the edge of the vessel and looked toward the east for the first blush of morning. The very first sunbeam, she knew, must kill her. She then saw her sisters rising out of the flood. They were as pale as herself, and their long and

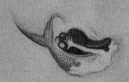

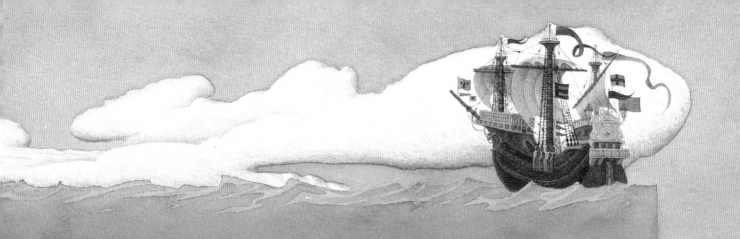

beautiful locks were no longer streaming to the winds, for they had been cut off.

"We gave them to the witch," said they, "to obtain help, that you might not die tonight. She gave us a knife in exchange—and a sharp one it is, as you may see. Now, before sunrise, you must plunge it into the prince's heart. And when his warm blood sprinkles your feet, they will again close up into a fish's tail, and you will be a mermaid once more and can come down to us and live out your three hundred years, before you turn into sea foam. Hurry, then! He or you must die before sunrise. Our old grandmother has fretted until her white hair has fallen off, as ours has under the witch's scissors. Hurry! Do you not see those red streaks in the sky? In a few minutes the sun will rise, and then you must die!" And together they sighed a deep, deep sigh, as they sank down into the waves.

The little mermaid lifted the scarlet curtain of the tent, and saw the beautiful bride resting her head on the prince's breast. The little mermaid bent down and kissed the prince's forehead, and she looked up at the heavens where the rosy dawn grew brighter and brighter. Then she gazed on the sharp knife, and again turned her eyes toward the prince, who was calling his bride by her name in his sleep. She alone filled his thoughts, and the mermaid's fingers clutched the knife instinctively—but in another moment she hurled the blade into the waves. It gleamed redly where it fell, as though drops of blood were gurgling up from the water. She gave the prince one last dying look, and then jumped overboard, and felt her body dissolving into foam.

The sun now rose out of the sea. Its beams threw a kindly warmth upon the cold foam, and the little mermaid did not experience the

pangs of death. She saw the bright sun, and above were floating hundreds of transparent, beautiful creatures. She could still catch a glimpse of the ship's white sails, and of the red clouds in the sky, across the swarms of these lovely beings. Their language was melody, but too ethereal to be heard by human ears, just as no human eye can discern their forms. Though they had no wings, their lightness poised them in the air. The little mermaid saw that she had a body like theirs, which kept rising higher and higher from out of the foam.

"Where am I?" she asked, and her voice sounded like that of her companions—so ethereal that no earthly music could give an adequate idea of its sweetness.

"Among the daughters of the air!" they answered. "A mermaid does not have an immortal soul, and cannot obtain one unless she wins the love of some human being—her eternal welfare depends on the will of another. But the daughters of the air, although not possessing an immortal soul by nature, can obtain one by their good deeds. We fly to warm countries, and fan the burning atmosphere, laden with pestilence, that destroys the sons of man. We diffuse the perfume of flowers through the air to heal and to refresh. When we have striven for many, many years to do all the good in our power, we then obtain an immortal soul, and share in the eternal happiness of the human race. You, poor little mermaid, have striven with your whole heart like ourselves. You have suffered and endured, and have raised yourself into an aerial spirit, and now your own good works may obtain you an immortal soul and entrance into Heaven."

And the little mermaid lifted her brightening eyes to the sun, and for the first time she felt them filled with tears. All was now astir in the ship, and she could see the prince and his beautiful bride looking for her, and then gazing sorrowfully at the pearly foam, as though they knew that she had cast herself into the waves. She kissed the bride's forehead and fanned the prince, unseen by either of them, and then mounted, together with the other daughters of the air, the rosy cloud that was sailing through the atmosphere.

AFTERWORD

In Denmark, more than one hundred fifty years ago, a promising young writer named Hans Christian Andersen published a small collection of fairy tales, which included "The Little Mermaid." He had based most of the stories on folk tales or historical legends. "The Little Mermaid," however, was an original creation. To his delight, this was the story that received the greatest acclaim, encouraging him to write many more tales that, to this day, captivate children and adults alike.

Since that time, there have been many translations and editions of "The Little Mermaid." Often, Andersen's prose or plot has been altered to make the story more suitable to the audience of the particular era. The Victorians made the language more proper as well as more flowery, thus robbing Andersen's story of its direct, straightforward charm. Several modern-day treatments have reduced the story to a short, superficial adventure with an upbeat ending, depriving the reader of the substance, tragedy, and full excitement of the complete work.

This edition presents the original story in all its wonder, essentially as it was translated in the mid-nineteenth century by Mary Howitt, a correspondent and friend of Andersen, who introduced his work to the English reading public. This graceful, elegant, and moving translation is considered by many to be the best of innumerable classic translations. In preparing the current edition, only the smallest adjustments have been made, in concession to contemporary pace and attitude, eliminating only some brief passages of heavily detailed description and moralizing.

Just as Andersen has had many translators down through the years, so has he also had many artistic interpreters, from the most obscure book illustrator to the famed English artist Arthur Rackham. But no one, perhaps, has so taken to heart the story of the soulful little mermaid as the distinguished American illustrator Charles Santore. As Santore has been moved by this touching story, so will readers be moved, as they revel in the magnificent color and detail, the emotion, and the fantasy that sweep across these pages.

Indeed, in this book, the magic of Hans Christian Andersen's story, brilliantly transcribed by Mary Howitt, is brought to its fullest visual realization by Charles Santore.

CLAIRE BOOSS
Editor

1993

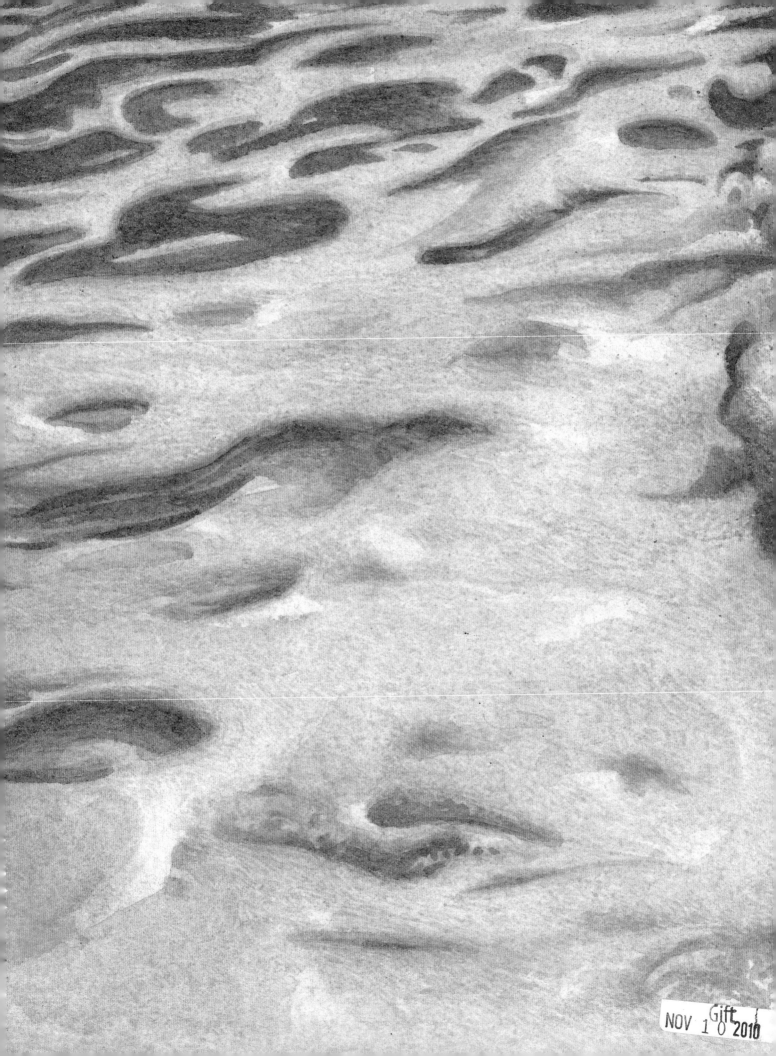